BUBBIE & RIVKA'S BEST-EVER CHALLAH (So Far!)

Sarah Lynne Reul

Abrams Books for Young Readers

New York

For my Grandma Ruth Zimmerman Cohen,
who always let me dress up in her costume jewelry.

Also, for my mom, Janet Cohen ("Bubbie" to my kids).
Thank you for baking your very first challah while testing
the recipe for this book. It was delicious!

The artwork for this book was drawn digitally in Photoshop. Sketches and shading were done with pencil on copy paper, then scanned and digitally incorporated into the final pieces.

Cataloging-in-Publication Data has been applied for and may be obtained from the Library of Congress.

ISBN 978-1-4197-5898-0

Text and illustrations © 2022 Sarah Lynne Reul
Book design by Heather Kelly

Published in 2022 by Abrams Books for Young Readers, an imprint of ABRAMS.

Printed and bound in China
10 9 8 7 6 5 4 3 2 1

Abrams Books for Young Readers are available at special discounts when purchased in quantity for premiums and promotions as well as fundraising or educational use. Special editions can also be created to specification. For details, contact specialsales@abramsbooks.com or the address below.

Abrams® is a registered trademark of Harry N. Abrams, Inc.

ABRAMS The Art of Books
195 Broadway, New York, NY 10007
abramsbooks.com

. . . *felt* so, so good

to **squish**

and **smoosh**

and **stretch**
and **squeeze**,

then **roll-pat** into long snakes

that Bubbie braided right up,
like my hair before bedtime.

It was Bubbie's first-ever challah too!

She's not the cooking kind of Bubbie . . . she's more of a
get-takeout-or-microwave-something kind of Bubbie.

"I know bupkis about baking. *Nothing!*"

Even though her *own* Bubbie used to make the best challah each and every week, *my* Bubbie has always been way too busy.

But now we have time, so we'll figure it out together. It's our new tradition: to make a challah every Friday!

Our first loaf was
flat and lumpy.
And pale!

We wondered what went wrong.

Did we knead the dough the right way?
Did we let it rise enough?
It was supposed to double in size, but it took a long, loooooooong time.

Too long! We didn't feel like waiting.

Maybe it needed a warmer spot?

And should we have baked it longer?

But never mind all that.
It was a good first try.
In fact, it was the best challah
that we'd ever made . . . so far!

As Mama always says, "Practice makes progress!"

The next week, we're back in the
kitchen and ready to go!

Bubbie takes off her rings and
places them on the sill of the
drafty old window.
I do the same.

Then we wash our hands with
warm water and lots of soap,
because nobody wants challah
with bits of dried paint!

This time, we try something different:
a new plan to help the dough rise.

While I **squish**
and **smoosh**

and **stretch**
and **squeeze**,

Bubbie warms the oven to low,
low, low then turns it OFF!

In goes the bowl with the just-mixed dough. It's not ready to bake yet! We just want it to be cozy and warm. This time, after an hour of waiting . . .

It's puffy!

At least twice as big as before.
"Now that's a good rise!" says Bubbie.

I poke and push and squish it back down, and she helps me split it into three sections.

To make sure our challah bakes all the way through, we set the timer for a couple extra minutes. But it turns into *way too many* minutes extra—since we forget to listen for the beep!

Oy gevalt.

At least it's not raw inside!

When we cut off the burnt stuff, there are still some good parts left.

And those taste . . . pretty good!

This loaf is definitely the best-ever challah so far.

"Crunchy," Grandpa grunts.

"Keep trying!" chirps Mama. Our best reviews yet!

The next week, Bubbie and I get down to business. We are experts now. Maybe even as good as *her* Bubbie!

Ingredients—**check!**

Warm place for rising—**check!**

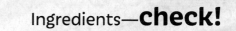

Oven timer—***double check!***

We set *two* separate timers
so we will hear them from
anywhere, no matter what!

We **squish**

and **smoosh**

and **stretch**

and **squeeze!**

We let our cozy dough rise, then we **roll-pat** it into ropes.

To make our challah shine, we brush extra egg all over the top of the braid, then pop it into the oven to bake.

The whole time, we're listening for the . . .

We dash to the kitchen with our
fingers crossed.
It smells so good!
How will *this* challah turn out?

Drumroll, please . . .
It's . . .

AMAZING!

All golden and gleaming, so hot that it's steaming!
Bubbie carefully lifts the loaf to let me
tap tap tap the bottom.
Does it sound hollow?

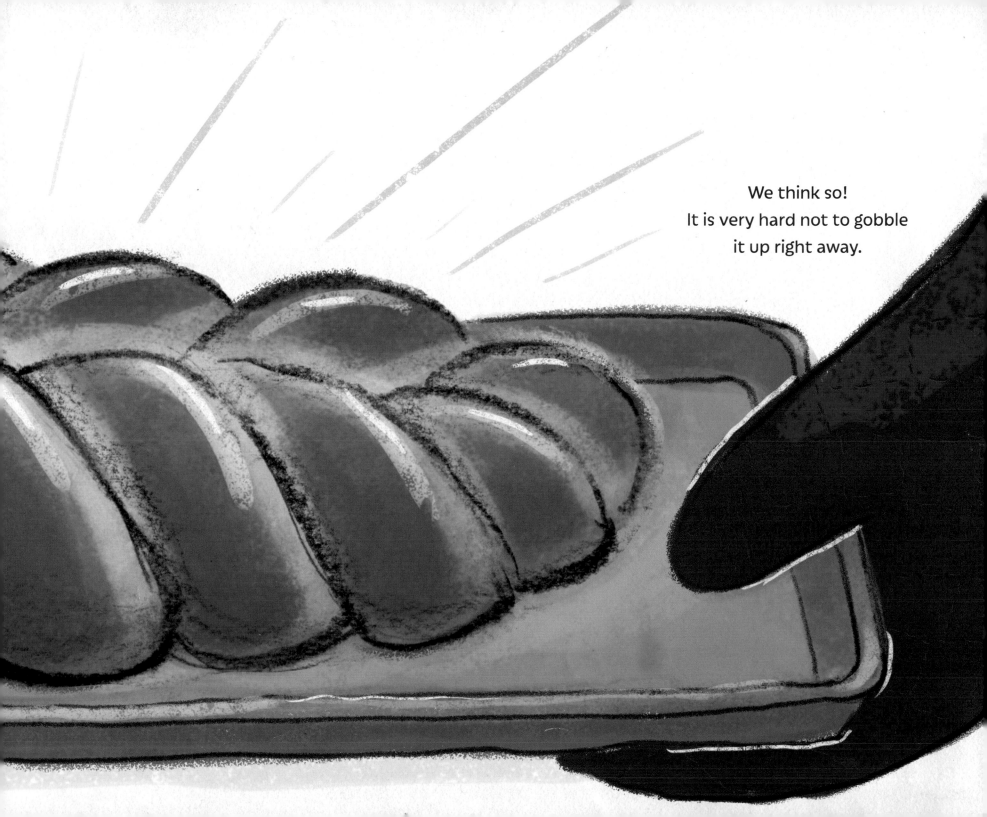

We think so!
It is very hard not to gobble
it up right away.

When we finally, finally share it, everyone
can tell that this challah is—

"the best-ever challah . . ."

". . . so far!"

CHALLAH

Makes 1 large loaf or 2 small loaves

Prep time: 45 minutes • Total rising time: 3–4 hours • Baking time: 25–30 minutes

Ingredients

- 3 eggs
- ¾ cup of warm water
- 2¼ teaspoons or one packet of active dry or instant yeast
- 3 tablespoons of sugar
- 3 tablespoons of vegetable or olive oil
- 2 teaspoons of salt
- 3½ cups of all-purpose or bread flour

Step 1: Mix

- Crack two of the eggs into a large bowl.
- Scramble with a fork or whisk.
- Add the water, yeast, sugar, oil, and salt to the egg until well mixed. Slowly stir in the flour until a dough forms.

Step 2: Knead

- Now it's time to squish and smoosh and stretch and squeeze! To knead the dough, plop it on a lightly floured surface. It will take about 10 to 15 minutes of folding, pushing, and turning with your hands to make the dough smoother and more elastic.
- If the dough is super sticky, you can sprinkle in more flour, a little at a time. But don't add more than another ½ cup.

Step 3: Rise #1

- Put the dough in a lightly oiled bowl (the oil will keep it from sticking). Cover with a damp, clean towel and set in a warm spot.

Tip: If your kitchen is chilly, you can try Bubbie's trick and warm the oven to its lowest setting (about 150°F), then turn it off and place the dough in the oven to rise.

- After 1 hour, check to see if the dough has just about doubled in size. Try to be patient—this could take up to 2 hours.

Step 4: Braid

- Separate the dough into 3 pieces of equal-ish size.
- Roll into long snakes, about 12 inches long. Braid the snakes together, squishing and tucking the ends underneath so they won't unravel.
- Place the braid on a baking sheet.

Tip: Line the pan with parchment paper for easier cleanup, or lightly oil the pan to prevent the loaf from sticking.

Step 5: Rise #2

- Crack the third egg into a small bowl, scramble, and then brush half of the egg mix over the braid. Leave the loaf uncovered to rise for another 45 minutes.
- While your dough is rising, preheat the oven to 375°F.
- Brush on the rest of the egg wash. This step will give your challah an extra-shiny crust!

Step 6: Bake

- Bake for 25 to 30 minutes.
- Take the challah out when it's golden brown.
- Tap the bottom to see if it sounds hollow.
- Enjoy your delicious challah nice and warm, or let it cool and slice it!

If you make this recipe a bunch of times, experiment with different ingredients! Sesame seeds can be sprinkled on top right before the loaf goes in the oven. Or try another delicious topping: "everything bagel" spice blend (with sesame seeds, poppy seeds, onion, garlic, and salt).

To get different flavors into the dough, try kneading in things like raisins or nuts or layering ingredients into the strands. To do this, flatten the 3 rolled snake pieces into long rectangles. Spread a filling onto the pieces, and then roll each piece up tightly before braiding together. For a savory loaf, try garlic and olives, or for something sweeter, slather on softened butter and sprinkle with cinnamon and sugar.

There are lots of ways to make challah. And remember: Practice makes progress!